R0084797257

02/2017

S0-AZK-088

The
Birthday Car

DEAR CAREGIVER,

The books in this Beginning-to-Read collection may look somewhat familiar in that the original versions could have been a part of your own early reading experiences. These carefully written texts feature common sight words to provide your child multiple exposures to the words appearing most frequently in written text. These new versions have been updated and the engaging illustrations are highly appealing to a contemporary audience of young readers.

Begin by reading the story to your child, followed by letting him or her read familiar words and soon your child will be able to read the story independently. At each step of the way, be sure to praise your reader's efforts to build his or her confidence as an independent reader. Discuss the pictures and encourage your child to make connections between the story and his or her own life. At the end of the story, you will find reading activities and a word list that will help your child practice and strengthen beginning reading skills. These activities, along with the comprehension questions are aligned to current standards, so reading efforts at home will directly support the instructional goals in the classroom.

Above all, the most important part of the reading experience is to have fun and enjoy it!

Shannon Cannon

Shannon Cannon,
Literacy Consultant

Norwood House Press • www.norwoodhousepress.com
Beginning-to-Read™ is a registered trademark of Norwood House Press.
Illustration and cover design copyright ©2017 by Norwood House Press. All Rights Reserved.

Authorized adapted reprint from the U.S. English language edition, entitled The Birthday Car by Margaret Hillert. Copyright © 2017 Pearson Education, Inc. or its affiliates. Reprinted with permission. All rights reserved. Pearson and The Birthday Car are trademarks, in the US and/or other countries, of Pearson Education, Inc. or its affiliates. This publication is protected by copyright, and prior permission to re-use in any way in any format is required by both Norwood House Press and Pearson Education. This book is authorized in the United States for use in schools and public libraries.

Designer: Lindaanne Donohoe
Editorial Production: Lisa Walsh

LIBRARY OF CONGRESS CATALOGING-IN-PUBLICATION DATA
  Names: Hillert, Margaret, author. | Girouard, Patrick, illustrator.
  Title: The birthday car / by Margaret Hillert ; illustrated by Patrick Girouard.
  Description: Chicago, IL : Norwood House Press, [2016] | Series: A
    beginning-to-read book | Originally published in 1966 by Follett
    Publishing Company. | Summary: "A boy receives a new red play car for his
    birthday and shares riding in it with his friends. Original edition
    revised with all new illustrations"-- Provided by publisher.
  Identifiers: LCCN 2016001872 (print) | LCCN 2016022129 (ebook) | ISBN
    9781599537955 (library edition : alk. paper) | ISBN 9781603579575 (eBook)
  Subjects: | CYAC: Automobiles--Fiction. | Toys--Fiction. | Birthdays--Fiction.
  Classification: LCC PZ7.H558 Bi 2016 (print) | LCC PZ7.H558 (ebook) | DDC
    [E]--dc23
  LC record available at https://lccn.loc.gov/2016001872

288N—072016
Manufactured in the United States of America in North Mankato, Minnesota.

The Birthday Car

A Beginning-to-Read Book

Illustrated by Patrick Girouard

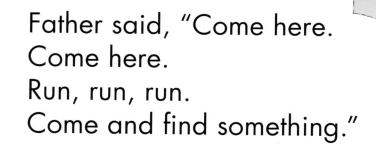

Father said, "Come here.
Come here.
Run, run, run.
Come and find something."

Father said, "Look, look.
Here is something for you."

Oh, oh, oh.
A little red car.

I can go.
I can go away.
Away, away, away.

Oh, my.
Oh, my.
See me.
It is fun.

I can go up.
Up, up, up.

I can come down.
Down, down, down.

Here is a little blue car.
Come and play.

Here is a little yellow car.
Come and play.
Come and play.

One, two, three cars.
Three little cars.
Red, yellow, and blue.

Three little cars can go.
Away, away, away.
Away we go.

Oh, look.
Here is something.
Something big.
Come and play.

Look here, look here.
Here is something little.
It can go.
Come and play.

See something.
Come and play.

Here we go.

We can go up.

We can go down.

We can go to my house.

Father, Father.
Here we come.

Father said, "Come in.
Come in."

Oh, oh, oh.
A little red car is fun.

Foundational Skills

In addition to reading the numerous high-frequency words in the text, this book also supports the development of foundational skills.

Phonological Awareness: The /b/ sound

Sound Substitution: Say the words on the left to your child. Ask your child to repeat the word, changing the first sound to **/b/**:

kite = bite	felt = belt	pat = bat	fun = bun
corn = born	fox = box	leak = beak	path = bath
goat = boat	turn = burn	mall = ball	glue = blue

Phonics: The Letter Bb

1. Demonstrate how to form the letters **B** and **b** for your child.
2. Have your child practice writing **B** and **b** at least three times each.
3. Ask your child to point to the words in the book that start with the letter **b**.
4. Write down the following words and ask your child to circle the letter **b** in each word:

bat	cab	barn	rub	cub	bird	bib	bed
baby	book	marble	bit	tub	crib	maybe	

Fluency: Shared Reading

1. Reread the story to your child at least two more times while your child tracks the print by running a finger under the words as they are read. Ask your child to read the words he or she knows with you.
2. Reread the story taking turns, alternating readers between sentences or pages.

Language

The concepts, illustrations, and text in this book help children develop language both explicitly and implicitly.

Vocabulary: Compound Words

1. Explain to your child that sometimes two words can be put together to make a new word. These are called compound words. The story has two compound words: birthday, and something.

28

2. Write down the following words on separate pieces of paper:

news	plane	board	base	bed	fly
box	butter	week	ball	paper	room
sand	air	house	skate	dog	end

3. Help your child move the pieces of paper around to form compound words.

Possible answers: newspaper, airplane, skateboard, baseball, bedroom, butterfly, sandbox, weekend, doghouse.

Reading Literature and Informational Text

To support comprehension, ask your child the following questions. The answers either come directly from the text or require inferences and discussion.

Key Ideas and Detail

- Ask your child to retell the sequence of events in the story.
- What other riding toys with wheels were there in this story?

Craft and Structure

- Is this a book that tells a story or one that gives information? How do you know?
- Do you think the boy in the story is friendly? Why or why not?

Integration of Knowledge and Ideas

- Why do you think this story is called "The Birthday Car"?
- How do you celebrate your birthday?

WORD LIST

The Birthday Car uses the 39 words listed below.

This list can be used to practice reading the words that appear in the text. You may wish to write the words on index cards and use them to help your child build automatic word recognition. Regular practice with these words will enhance your child's fluency in reading connected text.

a	go	oh	up
and		one	
away	here		we
	house	play	
big			yellow
blue	I	red	you
	in	run	
can	is		
car(s)	it	said	
come		see	
	little	something	
down	look		
		three	
Father	me	to	
find	my	two	
for			
fun			

ABOUT THE AUTHOR Margaret Hillert has helped millions of children all over the world learn to read independently. She was a first grade teacher for 34 years and during that time started writing books that her students could both gain confidence in reading and enjoy. She wrote well over 100 books for children just learning to read. As a child, she enjoyed writing poetry and continued her poetic writings as an adult for both children and adults.

Photograph by Glenna Washburn

ABOUT THE ILLUSTRATOR Patrick Girouard has created artwork for magazines, including Sesame Street Magazine, National Geographic World, Kid City, Spider, Weekly Reader and USA Today, to name a few. His work can be found on greeting cards, games, toys and puzzles, and in over one hundred books for children. Patrick's work has been exhibited at The Child at Heart Gallery and The Eric Carle Museum of Picture Book Art. www.pgirouard.com